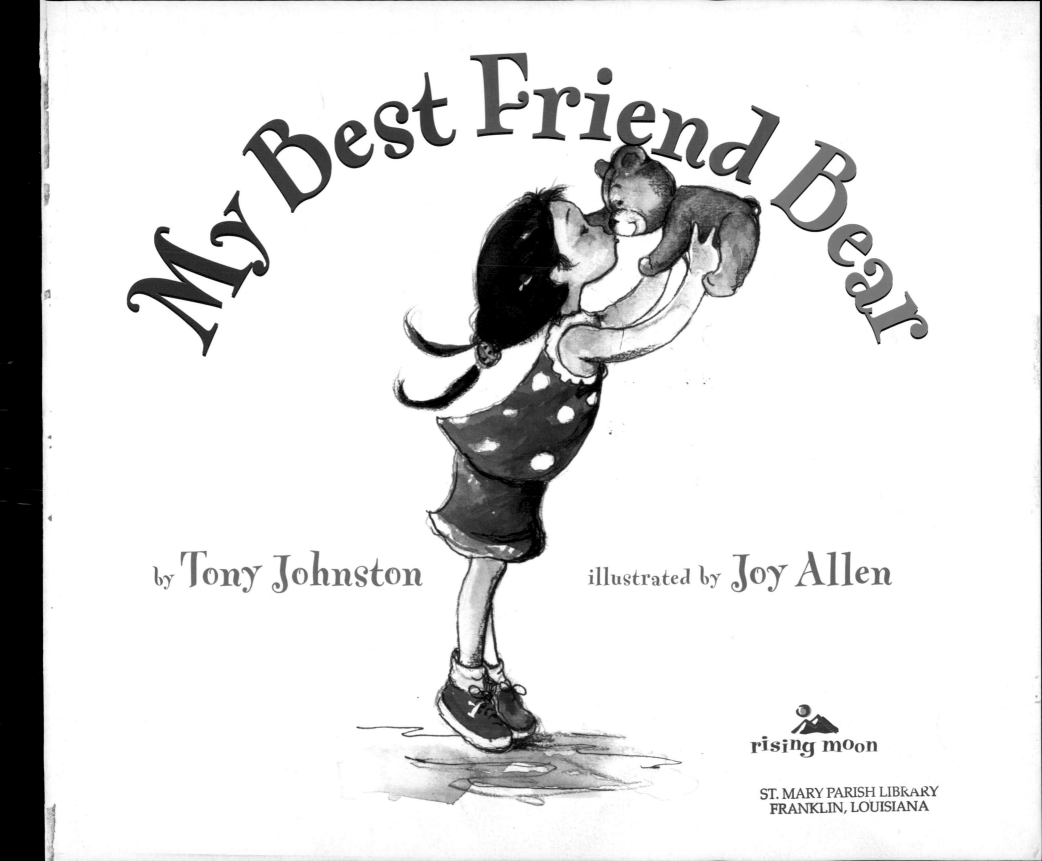

My Best Friend Bear

by **Tony Johnston**　　illustrated by **Joy Allen**

rising moon

The illustrations were rendered in pen and ink,
watercolor and colored pencil, then digitally enhanced.
The text and display type were set in Fontesque Text Regular
Composed in the United States of America
Designed by Lois A. Rainwater
Edited by Aimee Jackson
Production supervised by Lisa Brownfield

Printed in Hong Kong by Midas Printing, Ltd.

FIRST IMPRESSION
ISBN 0-87358-775-8
Library of Congress Catalog Card Number Pending

138/7.5M/3-01

For Cheedee-Darling, the greatest bear.

And for Ashley, who loves him.

—T. J.

For Curtis and his Teddy.

—J. A.

My old bear is my best friend.

Sometimes I tell him secrets.
Sometimes I tell him jokes.
Sometimes I read "The Three
Bears" to him. Sometimes we
dance the kookamonga
all around the house.

When I am in bed and
it is dark, my bear says,
"Piffle on the dark.
I am here, your
fierce friend, Bear."
And then I sleep.

When I am in bed and it is dark and
thunder rumbles, my bear says,
"Piffle on the dark. Poofle on the thunder.
I am here, your mighty friend, Bear."
And then I sleep.

My old bear is very old. I have told him so many secrets, his ears are gone. He has laughed at so many jokes, his mouth is gone. He has danced the kookamonga so gaily, his stuffing is all danced out.

Poor old Bear.

My old bear is very loved.
I love him. My dog loves him, too.
When I am looking somewhere else,
my dog takes him off to her little house.
She loves him so much, he is full of holes.

Poor old Bear.

One day Mother takes me
shopping. I take Bear. The
grocer smiles from behind the
counter and says,
"What a fine monkey."

Bear is so sad, he could cry.
But his eyes are gone.

Poor old Bear.

Mother says, "When bears
look like monkeys,
it's time to fix them."

If Bear had a mouth, he would say,

"Yes. And hurry, please."

Fixing a bear is the hardest job in the world.

First, you find the things you need to make him his good old self. Things like stuffing and buttons and fuzzy brown cloth and good, strong thread and a shiny, sharp needle.

Then what do you do?

You close your eyes to remember how Bear was when he was new. You make a picture of that.

Mother starts to sew, and you sit close and say "Yes" when things are yes and "No" when they're not. You show her your picture again and again. That way she won't make a strange bear that you don't know.

Mother sticks the needle in and slips it out again. The holes close up. The body grows fat. Then come ears, legs, arms. Then the face is there.

And…

There is fierce and mighty Bear!

Because Bear has been so brave,

Mother sews a heart on him, too.

Then what do you do?

You wash him gently and
hang him out to dry.
And THEN what do you do?

You stay while he dries
and eat a sandwich and
shoo the birds away—
in case he looks like stuff
for a nest.
Soon the sun does its job.

Mother takes Bear off the line.
He looks fine.
And THEN what do
you do?

You kiss him and say,
"Hello, Bear. I'm glad you're back."
He says, "I am, too."
"Thank you very much," you both say to Mother.
And you dance the kookamonga
all around the house.

TONY JOHNSTON has written over one-hundred books for young people. She has won many awards for her work, including the 1997 Simon Wiesenthal Center Award for children's tolerance literature for *The Wagon*. Mrs. Johnston's struggles with needle and thread to repair her daughter Ashley's bear, Cheedee-Darling, was the inspiration for this book. (Cheedee-Darling is alive and well and in a most excellent state of repair.)

JOY ALLEN began illustrating picture books in 1997 after a long career in graphic design. She has been profiled in *Children's Writer's & Illustrator's Market*, and was featured as editor's choice in *Art Gallery Magazine*. Some of her most recent picture books include: *Mud Pie Annie* and *Hold The Boat*. Illustrating *My Best Friend Bear* brought back great memories for Ms. Allen who has a "bear friend" of her own (pictured above).